Starla Jean

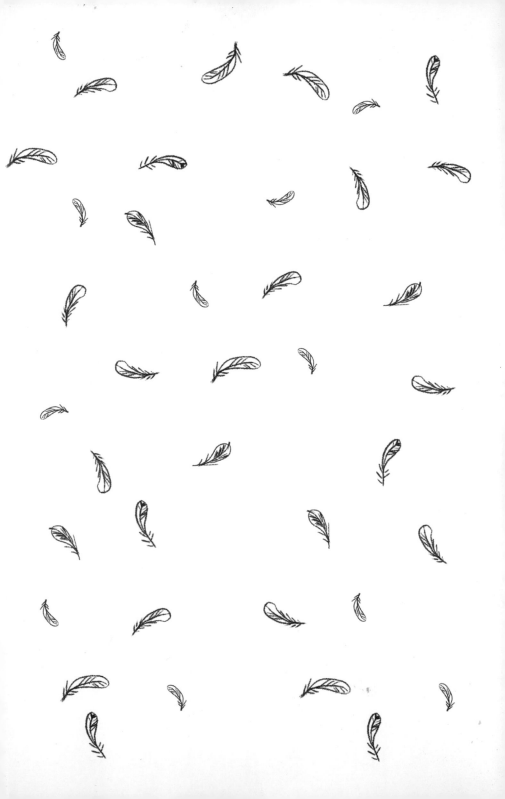

Starla Jean

WHICH CAME FIRST:
THE CHICKEN OR THE FRIENDSHIP?

ELANA K. ARNOLD   Illustrated by **A. N. KANG**

ROARING BROOK PRESS
NEW YORK

Library of Congress Control Number: 2020912184
ISBN: 978-1-250-30576-3
Our books may be purchased in bulk for promotional, educational,
or business use. Please contact your local bookseller or the Macmillan
Corporate and Premium Sales Department at (800) 221-7945 ext. 5442 or
by email at MacmillanSpecialMarkets@macmillan.com.

First edition, 2021
Book design by Aram Kim
Printed in China by Toppan Leefung Printing Ltd.,
Dongguan City, Guangdong Province

3   5   7   9   10   8   6   4   2

FOR MAX ARNOLD, THE ORIGINAL
CHICKEN-CATCHING EXPERT. —E.K.A.

FOR MY BFF, MICHELLE! —A.K.

CONTENTS

CHAPTER THREE

Winner, Winner, Chicken...Dinner?

CHAPTER FOUR

House Chicken

CHAPTER ONE

If You Can Catch It, You Can Keep It

There are certain things you have to do if you're going to catch a chicken.

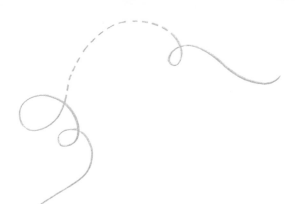

Trust me. I'm an expert.

I wasn't always a chicken-catching expert.

Until last Thursday, I didn't know much about chickens at all.

These are the things I *did* know:

Chickens lay eggs that people like to eat. (My favorite way to eat a chicken egg is sunny-side up, with two pieces of toast.)

Chickens, like all birds, have feathers and wings, but chickens can't fly.

 Chickens like to take dust baths.

Chickens aren't very smart.

It turned out that not everything I knew about chickens was true.

Last Thursday, I went to the park with my dad. We rode there on our double bicycle, like we always do.

We rode through the neighborhood,

waving to Mr. Marcos and Dean, who were watering the lawn together. "Good day, Starla Jean," Mr. Marcos said.

We said hello to Jules and her mom, who were counting roly-poly bugs.

We went up and over the bridge, and there was Dani, looking for treasure again.

"Maybe today will be your lucky day!" Dad called to her.

We parked the double bike near the swings. I love swinging, but all three were taken.

Dad sat down with his book and a sandwich in the shade of the willow tree. I wasn't ready to sit down yet.

I walked around and looked at things. I looked at the hard,

old roots of the trees. I looked at the soft, wet leaves tucked between them. And then I heard a sound—

AAAAAAW

BAWK!

It was the skinniest, ugliest chicken I had ever seen!

The chicken walked over to the soft, wet leaves, her skinny neck jutting out with each step. And then she scratched at the dirt with her claws—

SCRITCH
SCRATCH
SCRITCH!

—until she found a worm, which she snapped up in her sharp orange beak.

"Dad!" I called. I didn't move from my spot. I didn't look away from the chicken. "Dad, look!"

He walked over. His shadow stretched over me and the chicken, who didn't seem to notice.

SCRITCH
SCRATCH
SCRITCH!

"That's a chicken!" he said. He sounded as surprised as I felt.

"I think it's lost," I said. "Chickens don't belong in the park. Can we take it home with us?"

"If you can catch it, you can keep it!" Dad said. He was laughing, like he didn't really think I could do it.

And that was when I knew I was
going to catch a chicken.

CHAPTER TWO

Found Chicken

Do you remember how I told you that before last Thursday, I knew four things about chickens? And how I said that of those four things, only some of them turned out to be true?

It turns out that chickens *can* fly! Not very far, but pretty fast. And it turns out that chickens are way smarter than they look.

"You've got to be smarter than the chicken, Starla Jean," Dad said in his teasing voice. He didn't seem to think I would be bringing the chicken home that day.

BAAAAWWWK!

I guess Dad was wrong about some of the things *he* had thought, too.

And that's the story of how I caught myself a chicken.

The whole way home, I tried to help the chicken feel more comfortable.

The first thing I did was give her a name. That way she would know that we weren't going to eat her. After all, you don't name your food.

"We will call you Opal Egg," I told Opal Egg.

"Opal Egg?" Dad looked like he wasn't sure about that name.

But I was. "Yes," I said. "Her name
is Opal Egg."

And once she had a name, Opal Egg *did* seem less nervous.

Dad, on the other hand, seemed more and more nervous the closer we got to home.

"I never thought she would catch that chicken," I heard him say softly.

"That sure is a nice chicken, Starla Jean," said Mr. Marcos.

"*Woof*," said Dean.

"Thank you, Mr. Marcos. Thank you, Dean," I said.

"I never thought she would catch that chicken," Dad said again.

"Starla Jean can do anything she puts her mind to," said Mr. Marcos.

Now Dad looked even *more* nervous.

Mom opened the door when we got home. "Shhh . . . Willa is sleeping," she said. Then she said, "Starla Jean, is that a *chicken*?"

"I never thought she would catch that chicken," Dad said, "but I should have known better. Starla Jean can do anything she puts her mind to."

We sat at the kitchen table. I told Mom all about how I caught Opal Egg and how I gave her a name so that she would be more comfortable.

"Because you don't give a name to your dinner," I explained.

Mom folded laundry and listened.
Dad folded laundry and shook his
head.

Finally, Mom said, "Starla Jean, I think it's great that you caught that chicken. A park is no place for a chicken. But don't you think she must belong to somebody? A nice chicken like that?"

Actually, I had been thinking the very same thing, even though

I tried not to. "Yes," I said sadly.
"She must be somebody's chicken."

Dad stopped looking so worried.
"We'll make posters!" he said. And
he rushed off to find cardboard and
markers.

"Should we put a picture of her?" I asked.

"I think anyone who lost a chicken will call us," Mom said. "It's not every day you lose a chicken."

"It's not every day you *find* a chicken," I said.

BAWK! said Opal Egg, as if she agreed with me.

CHAPTER THREE

Winner, Winner, Chicken...Dinner?

"I'll go hang up these signs right now," Dad said.

"Starla Jean," Mom said, "how about putting the chicken in the backyard?"

"Her name is Opal Egg," I told Mom.

"How about putting Opal Egg in the backyard?" Mom said. And then she said, "Oh, dear. I hear your sister. That was a short nap."

Mom went to get Willa. Willa is a baby. Babies are okay. But they aren't as good as chickens.

"I'll bet you're hungry," I said to Opal Egg.

BAWK! said Opal Egg.

I didn't know what chickens liked to eat.

So I decided to find out.

I learned something else about chickens. My list of chicken facts now included:

Chickens lay eggs that people like to eat. (My favorite way to eat a chicken egg is sunny-side up, with two pieces of toast.)

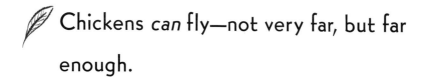 Chickens *can* fly—not very far, but far enough.

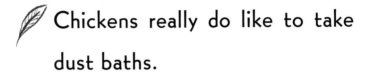 Chickens really do like to take dust baths.

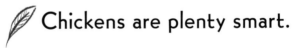 Chickens are plenty smart.

Chickens like to eat *a lot* of different foods.

"Starla Jean!" Mom said. "What on earth is that chicken doing on the kitchen table?"

"Opal Egg is eating dinner," I said.

"On the kitchen table?"

"That's where *we* eat dinner," I said.

"*Exactly*," Mom said.

BAWK!

BAWK! said Opal Egg.

"Bawk!" said Willa.

"I hung up all the signs," said Dad,

slamming the front door. He didn't look worried anymore *at all*.

"Did you say *bawk*?" Mom asked Willa.

"Bawk!" said Willa again.

"Starla Jean!" Mom said. "That chicken taught your sister her first word!"

"Her name," I said, "is Opal Egg."

CHAPTER FOUR

House Chicken

Mom was glad that Opal Egg had taught Willa a word.

But she still didn't think Opal Egg belonged inside the house.

"Chickens aren't house pets," Mom said.

But if a chicken is in the house and you pet it, then doesn't that make it a house pet?

"Chickens poop too much to be house pets," Mom said.

"Willa poops all the time," I said, "and you let *her* live in the house."

"That's different," Mom said.

Mom was right. It was different. "I'll be right back," I said.

Maybe Opal Egg wouldn't get to stay with us for very long. But while she was here, I wanted her to feel at home.

The doorbell rang, but I was too busy to answer it. I heard Dad go to the door. From the kitchen, I heard Willa. "Bawk!" she said.

"Can you say *Mama*?" Mom asked.

"There," I said. I picked up Opal Egg. I carried her back to the kitchen.

"Now she's a house chicken!" I said.

"Starla Jean," Dad called from the door. "You have a visitor."

"Starla Jean!" said Dani. "You found my chicken!"

"*Your* chicken?" I felt like I might cry.

"Well, one of my chickens," Dani said. "I have seven. But this one keeps running away. The bigger chickens pick on her, poor thing."

BAWK! said Opal Egg.

"Bawk!" said Willa.

I set Opal Egg back on the kitchen table. She was still hungry.

"Starla Jean," Dani said, "is that a ... diaper?"

"Yes," I said. "It's Willa's."

"And ... is all that food for the chicken?" Dani asked.

"Her name is Opal Egg," I said. "I named her Opal Egg."

"That's a good name," Dani said. "It sounds like a treasure."

"She is a treasure," I said, "to me."

"Starla Jean," said Dani, "it sounds like *you're* a treasure ... for Opal Egg."

"Dani," said Dad. He looked worried again. "Starla Jean sure has gotten attached to that chicken . . . to Opal Egg."

"Bawk," said Willa.

"Starla Jean," Dani said, "how would you like to keep that chicken?"

"*Keep* Opal Egg?"

"Yes," said Dani.

"She can sleep outside," Mom said. "We can build her a coop."

BAWK BAWK BAWK BAWK BAWK BAWK BAWK BAWK

Well, that was last Thursday. Since then, Opal Egg and I have hunted for snails in the garden (she thinks they're delicious), we've played in the sandbox, we've read books in my room, and we've even taught Willa another word.

Fun Facts about Chickens

🪶 Chickens use the sun to tell what time it is.

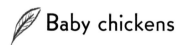 Chickens can do math! They can

add and subtract small numbers.

 Baby chickens

are born with

a tooth on their

beak that they use to break out

of the egg.

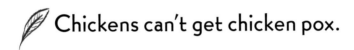 Chickens can't get chicken pox.

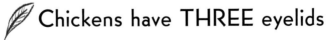 Chickens have THREE eyelids

on each eye!

Chickens enjoy sitting on a swing.

Most chickens have four toes on each foot . . . but some have five!

Don't Miss

. . . Willa likes Opal Egg, too. But it's my job to keep an eye on them. Because if she gets a chance, Willa is a tail-grabbing feather-puller.

So I was watching Willa and she was watching Opal Egg and Opal Egg was doing some gardening—

SCRITCH

SCRATCH

SCRITCH!

—when we heard another sound, definitely not a chicken sound.

MEOW
MEOW
MEOOOW

To be continued in *Starla Jean Takes the Cake!*

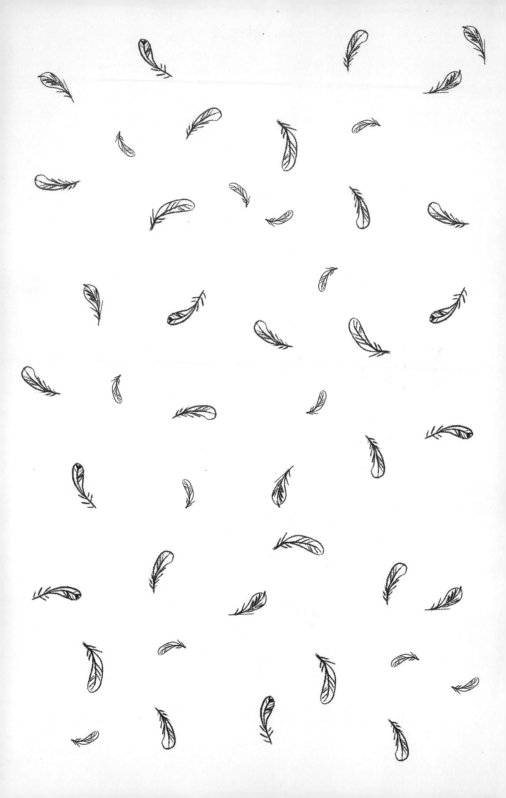